To Elizabeth and Tanya, my sister bear cubs. –K. N.

For Sarah, Amy, and Tracey. –L. W.

STERLING CHILDREN'S BOOKS
New York

An Imprint of Sterling Publishing Co., Inc.
1166 Avenue of the Americas
New York, NY 10036

ISBN 978-1-4549-1610-9

Distributed in Canada by Sterling Publishing Co., Inc.
c/o Canadian Manda Group, 664 Annette Street
Toronto, Ontario, Canada M6S 2C8
Distributed in the United Kingdom by GMC Distribution Services
Castle Place, 166 High Street, Lewes, East Sussex, England BN7 1XU

For information about custom editions, special sales, and premium and corporate purchases,
please contact Sterling Special Sales at 800-805-5489 or
specialsales@sterlingpublishing.com.

Manufactured in China

Lot #:
2 4 6 8 10 9 7 5 3 1
07/16

www.sterlingpublishing.com

The artwork for this book was created
using watercolor, colored pencil, and pastel.
Designed by Andrea Miller
and Igor Satanovsky

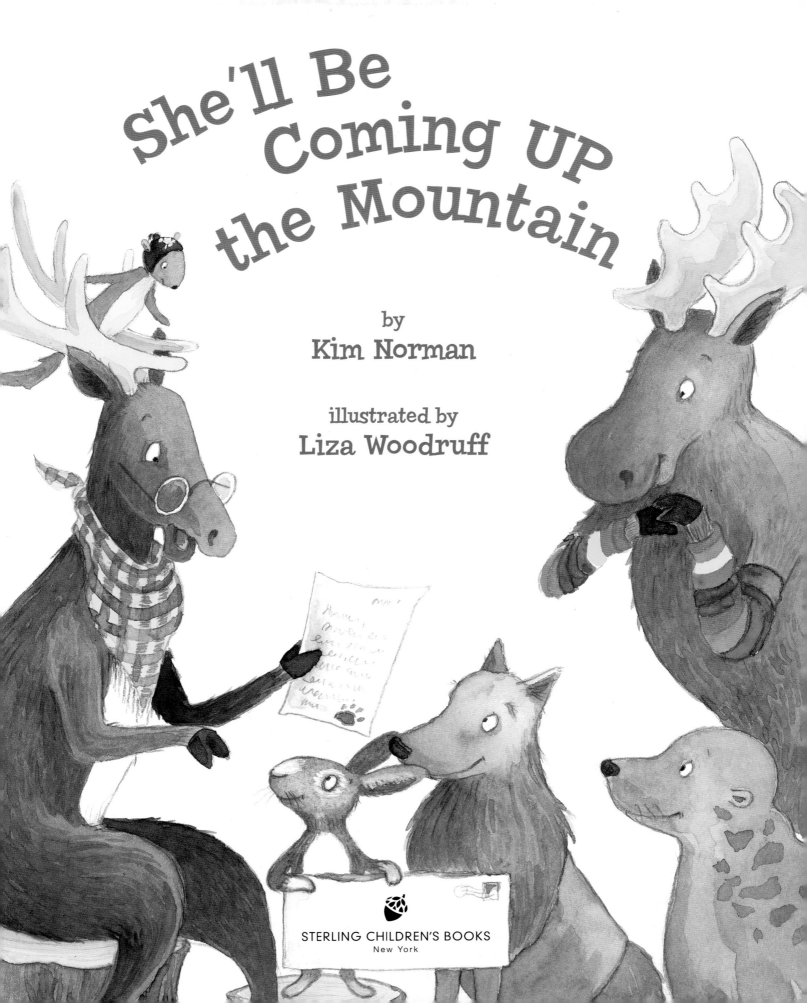

She'll Be Coming UP the Mountain

by
Kim Norman

illustrated by
Liza Woodruff

STERLING CHILDREN'S BOOKS
New York

She'll be coming up the mountain when she comes.
She'll enjoy our frozen fountain when she comes.
We will playfully hello her
and have lots we'll want to show her.

She'll be just the way we know her when she comes.

We were sorry when she left us in the fall.
But she always kept her promise that she'd call.
When she gets here she'll discover
just how much we really love her
in a banner strung along the cabin wall.

We are certain that we made it very clear
that we think about her when she isn't near:
We sent poems in a letter,
even knitted her a sweater,

but we'll all be feeling better when she's here.

Even narwhals will salute her when she comes.
Cheering friends will all uproot her when she comes.
Overhead the gulls will natter,
as our teeth begin to chatter.

Not a bit of that will matter when she comes.

We will plan an arctic party when she comes.
We'll play music, tapping icicles and drums.
Everybody will be clapping
while the caribou is rapping.

Not a creature will be napping when she comes.

It will be a big vacation when she's here.
We will kayak in formation when she's here.
We'll be shivering and shouting
while the humpback whales are spouting,
so there won't be any doubting that she's here.

We will cover her in gifts when she arrives.

Then we'll slap our paws, high-ones and twos and fives.

She'll be playful as an otter
when she's swimming underwater,
as she models what we bought her for her dives.

We will try out something daring when she comes.
She will whoop at what we're wearing when she comes.
We'll take photos that are cheesy.
even when it's one-degree-zy.
We will all be breathing easy when she comes.

When we message her, she instantly replies,
and she tells us that we won't believe our eyes.
Should we send our fastest skier,
who will be the first to see her,
and can tell us what will be her big surprise?

We hear snuffles in a snowbank, drawing near,
so we know that any second she'll appear.

Now we're bouncing off each rafter,
as we hear her roaring laughter.
We are happy ever after . . .